Jolie Jones
Little Kisses

Illustrated by **Julie Downing**

The Julie Andrews Collection

HarperCollins**Publishers**

Library of Congress Cataloging-in-Publication Data
Jones, Jolie.
   Little Kisses / Jolie Jones ; illustrated by Julie Downing. — 1st ed.
     p.   cm. — (The Julie Andrews collection)
   Summary: A dog named Bejinhos, or "Little Kisses," enjoys the time he
spends with his owner, Jolie, and other children and pets of their neighbor-
hood, even though there are many rules to follow.
   ISBN-10: 0-06-058698-2 — ISBN-10: 0-06-058699-0 (lib. bdg.)
   ISBN-13: 978-0-06-058698-0 — ISBN-13: 978-0-06-058699-7 (lib. bdg.)
   1. Dogs—Juvenile Fiction. [1. Dogs—Fiction. 2. Pets—Fiction.
3. Neighborhood—Fiction. 4. Rules (Philosophy)—Fiction.] I. Downing, Julie, ill.
II. Title. III. Series.
PZ10.3.J755Li 2006   2004019107
[E]—dc22   CIP
                                        AC

Typography by Jeanne L. Hogle
1 2 3 4 5 6 7 8 9 10
❖
First Edition

This book is dedicated to Fireball and Mr. Bunny.
In loving memory of Vanya and the Crazy Pelican.
—J.J.

To Molly
—J.D.

My Jolie loves me so much!
When I'm sleeping, she gives me little kisses.
"I love you, Bejinhos—you're such a good boy."
That makes me feel good!

She named me Bejinhos because it means little kisses in Brazil. Jolie means pretty in France, and she says one day we'll get to go there!

My Jolie is the prettiest girl in the world!

I give little kisses to her in the morning. She smiles and we have a little cuddle. Her bed is soft and fluffy.

"No jumping on the bed. Those are the rules," she says.

My Jolie and I get up, and we talk. We talk about everything . . .

feelings . . . friends . . . what we'll do today and what we'll wear.

She has her cocoa while I eat my breakfast. Food gets all over the floor. She loves me anyway.

We brush our teeth after breakfast. "Those are the rules," says My Jolie.

The best part of the day is our walk.

Up to the village, down to the bluffs.

That is where Nani lives.

Nani means beautiful in Hawaii.

Nani runs to meet us.

My Jolie's friend Dotsie comes too.

From here we can see way down to the pier
and way up the coast.

The ocean is so big and blue. We see
boats and dolphins playing.

Dotsie gives us treats.

"Never take treats from strangers.
Those are the rules," says Dotsie.

I have *lots* of
friends. On one
corner is my best
friend, Kibawa. His
name means little
brother in Africa.

Then on another
corner is Tess. When I
stop at a corner, I wait
until My Jolie says,
"Okay . . . let's go!"
Then we cross. Those
are the rules.

We see Pinky and Linky walking with their father.

He looks at the heart-shaped charm I wear with my name on it. "That's a big name for a little guy! How do you say that?"

"Bejinhos . . . the beginning sounds just like the color beige," says My Jolie. "You can call him Little Kisses. It's okay."

Then he says, "Hi, Little Kisses!"

Guess what the father does at the corner?

He stops and looks both ways and says,

"Okay! It's safe to cross. The light is green."

My Jolie isn't the only one with rules.

Kibawa is watching while I walk

across with my head held high.

It's fun having friends!

We walk together for a
while and then go home.
When we get there, My Jolie
says, "It's schooltime now,
Little Kisses. I have to go.
You stay in the yard and
be a good boy! Those are
the rules!"

I wish I could go to school!

I roll in the grass.
I take a little nap.

When I wake up, I chase a
pretty butterfly.

I find one of my
toys stuck under a
rock near the
fence.
I try to dig it out.

I dig and I dig and
I dig some more.

Then I feel something really
hard. So I crawl into the hole
to dig around it.

I end up somewhere cold, dark . . . and scary!

I start to cry.

I'm a big boy, but sometimes I cry.

My Jolie says there are no rules about that!

Before I can turn around, I am
face-to-face with the neighborhood
bully, Titus!

It's really hard to run
looking backwards!

It's getting dark and I don't know
where my house is.

Oh, no! I'm lost!

Next thing I know, I see headlights!

Brakes screech!

I am shaking and my heart is pounding.

I want My Jolie!

"Little Kisses! I've been looking everywhere for you and I've been so worried! You didn't follow the rules!" she says with tears in her eyes.

My Jolie picks me up.
"You were very naughty," she says.
I give My Jolie little kisses.
"All right, I know you will
follow the rules from
now on. I love you,
Bejinhos," she says.

That makes me feel good!